This Little Tiger
book belongs to:

_____

_____

_____

For Olivia Grace, with love ~ M C B

For my father, Alan R Macnaughton ~ T M

LITTLE TIGER PRESS LTD,
an imprint of the Little Tiger Group
1 Coda Studios
189 Munster Road, London SW6 6AW
www.littletiger.co.uk

First published in Great Britain 2006
This edition published 2018

CD contains:
1 - complete story with original music and sound effects
2 - story with page turn pings to encourage learner readers to join in

Running time over 15 mins
Produced by Matinée Sound & Vision Ltd
Music composed by Steven Houlsby
Story read by Justin Fletcher and Sophie Thompson

ISBN 978-1-78881-077-7
LTP/2700/2946/0719
Printed in China
10 9 8 7 6 5 4 3 2

One Winter's Day

M Christina Butler

Tina Macnaughton

LITTLE TIGER

LONDON

Little Hedgehog was making his bed for the winter when a sudden gust of wind blew him off his feet. It took hold of his cosy nest and tossed it high into the air.

Little Hedgehog trembled as the wind whistled around him, and he wondered what to do.

He caught hold of his scarf, hat and mittens before they blew away, and tried to shelter under the tree roots. But wherever he went the wind was there as well.

"I'll have to stay with Badger until this storm
has gone," he said at last, pulling his woolly
hat firmly over his prickles. Then he snuggled
into his cosy scarf, put on his mittens and,
with a deep breath, he set off.

The wind was even stronger in the
meadow. Leaves swirled here and there,
and snowflakes filled the air.

Little Hedgehog hadn't gone far when he bumped into a family of field mice shivering in the long grass.

"I've never known such a storm!" squeaked
Mother Mouse. "The wind has blown our nest
far away, and my poor babies are so cold."

"My home has been blown away as well,"
said Little Hedgehog. "I'm on my way to stay
with Badger, but I have just the thing to warm
you up!" And he took off his woolly hat and
gave it to the mice.

"Ooh! Lovely, lovely," they squeaked,
snuggling down out of the wind.
"Thank you, Little Hedgehog!"

Little Hedgehog tucked his nose inside his scarf and ran along beside the racing river. Otter was on the bank, huffing and puffing on his paws.

"Hello, Otter!" shouted Little Hedgehog. "What are you doing?"

"Oh hello, Hedgehog," replied Otter. "My fur coat keeps me warm but my paws are freezing!"

"Here, have these," said Little Hedgehog, giving Otter his mittens. "They should do the trick!"

"Thank you, Little Hedgehog!" said Otter. "These are great! But shouldn't you be at home in this cold weather?"

"I have no home any more," Little Hedgehog replied sadly. "The wind has blown it away." And running on, he cried, "I'm going to stay with Badger!"

By the time Little Hedgehog reached the wood the snow was getting deeper. On and on he struggled, picking his way between the snowdrifts as the wind howled around him.

A mother deer and her fawn were sheltering in the bushes. "Oh Little Hedgehog, why aren't you in your nest in this awful storm?" she asked.

So Little Hedgehog told Mother Deer about his nest blowing away. But as he spoke he saw that the little fawn was shaking with cold.

"Here, take this," he said, giving the fawn his scarf.

"How kind you are," said Mother Deer. "Thank you, Little Hedgehog."

Little Hedgehog pattered on, faster and faster.
But just as he finally saw Badger's house at the
bottom of the hill, he skidded on the icy path.
  "Help!" he cried as he went bumping and
bouncing through the snow.

Badger was making tea when he heard a big THUD! outside. "Whatever was that?" he cried, dropping his toast.

When he opened the door a prickly snowball rolled in. "Gracious me!" he said in surprise. "It's Little Hedgehog!"

Badger carried Little Hedgehog to an
armchair by the fire and gave him a cup
of tea. Little Hedgehog told Badger about
his journey through the storm and then,
cosy and warm, he fell fast asleep.

Little Hedgehog stayed with Badger until the storm had gone. As they walked to where his house had been Little Hedgehog was very worried. "How can I build a strong new nest if all the leaves and twigs have blown away and there's nothing left?" he asked anxiously.

"I'll help you," said Badger kindly. "We're nearly there now."

"Surprise!" came the cry when they turned
the corner. Little Hedgehog gasped with delight.
The animals he'd met in the storm had made
him the cosiest nest he'd ever seen.

"For the kindest hedgehog in the world!"
they all cried together.

More fabulous books
from Little Tiger Press!

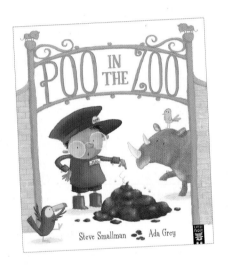

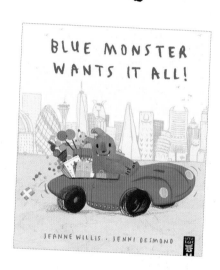

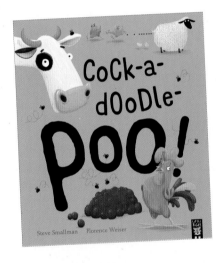

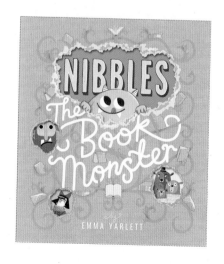

For information regarding any of the above books or for our catalogue, please contact us:
Little Tiger Press Ltd, 1 Coda Studios, 189 Munster Road, London SW6 6AW
Tel: 020 7385 6333 • E-mail: contact@littletiger.co.uk • www.littletiger.co.uk